Amy and Ken Visit Grandma

Written and illustrated by Akiko Hayashi

Translated by Peter Howlett and Richard McNamara

R.I.C. Publications
Dublin • London • Perth • Tokyo

Ken sat waiting for the new baby to arrive. Grandma, who lives in Dunetown, had sent Ken to look after the newborn baby.

"Ahhh …" yawned Ken. "I'm so tired of sitting around here and just waiting. I wish I could go back to Dunetown. It would be so good to see Grandma again," thought Ken.

He dozed off, and in his dreams the great sand dunes spread out before him.

Ken heard a voice and then, after a long silence, the sound of a music box. He woke up and, to his surprise, there was the baby.

"The baby's arrived! How tiny and cute a baby is!" thought Ken. He was so excited his heart was pounding.

The baby's name was Amy. Amy sometimes dribbled all over his hand.

When Amy learned to crawl she would sometimes crawl all over him too.

The first day she wore shoes, she walked dragging Ken by his tail.

Ken didn't mind, however, for he loved to play with Amy. They played together every day and Amy grew up to become a little girl. But as Amy grew up, Ken grew older and …

… one day his arms came apart at the seams.

"I'm all right. I'm all right," said Ken.

"But I think I'll have to go to Grandma's to get her to mend me," he said. He was just about to go when Amy begged, "Please, let me go with you!"—and she got ready to go too.

Ken and Amy arrived at the station.

"This is the train to get on, Amy. Just follow me," said Ken as he got on the train.

Before they could get seated, the train pulled out of the station with a jerk .

"That's our seat over there," said Ken.

Ken jumped onto the empty seat and said, "Amy, you can sit next to the window and watch the view if you like. Now, just sit there and before you know it we will arrive at Grandma's station."

"But what if we get hungry?" asked Amy.

"No problem, at the next station they sell a wonderful box lunch," said Ken. The train stopped and Ken hurried out to buy the box lunches.

"Wait for me!" shouted Amy, a little worried.

"Amy, just wait here. The train's going to stop for five minutes so there's lots of time to buy our lunches," said Ken.

But by the time Ken got out, there was a long line of people in front of the box lunch stand.

Ken became a bit worried.

"Oh dear, there's only three minutes left," he said
to himself.

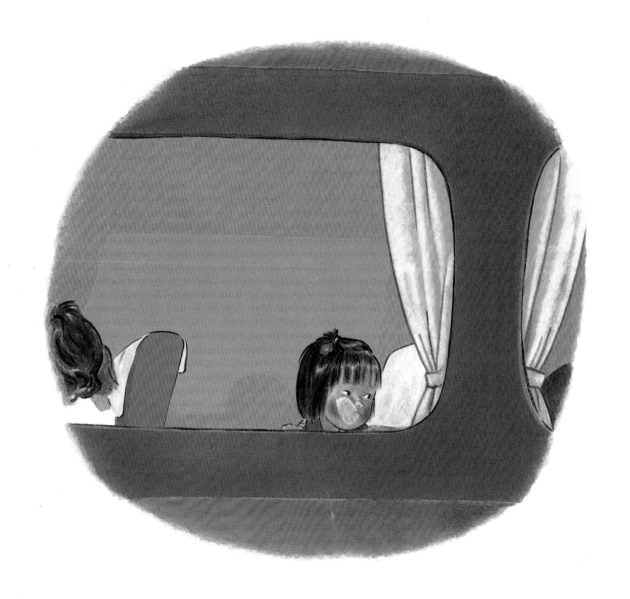

Ken didn't return for a long time and Amy's heart began to pound.

The doors closed and the train started to pull out.

Amy waited and waited but Ken didn't return. Just then the conductor came by to check the passengers' tickets. Amy told him about her missing friend, Ken.

"If it's a Mr Fox you're talking about, I saw him standing next to the door," said the conductor.

Amy rushed to the door and, sure enough, there next to the door was Ken. He had two box lunches in his hand and seeing Amy's upset face he said, "I'm all right. I'm all right. And look, our box lunches are still warm."

Ken had jumped on the train at the very last moment and his tail had got caught in the door.

Ken and Amy started to eat their lunches when the conductor came by again and said, "Well, surprise! Now, why are you two eating your lunches here?"

Taking their tickets out of his pocket, Ken explained, "I'm not trying to hide from you, sir, here's our tickets. It's just that my tail's caught in the door."

Finally, the door opened at the next station and Ken's tail came free.

But his mid-tail was squashed flat.

After they returned to their seats, the conductor came by to bandage Ken's tail.

"Ken, let's just stay put, okay?" said Amy.

"Yes, let's," answered Ken and they both sat and stared out the window and watched the countryside fly by. They sat and sat until …

… finally, they reached their destination: Dunetown Station.

"It's this way to Grandma's and that way to the sand dunes," explained Ken.

"Ken, do you think we could just take a quick look at the sand dunes?"

"Sure, but let's just make a few footprints and then be on our way."

This was the first time Amy had seen the sand dunes.

Amy and Ken made footprints in the sand.

"Look Ken!" said Amy. "Whose footprints are these?"

"I wonder …" said Ken, and they both started to follow them.

Suddenly, from out of the pine grove a dog came scampering across the sand. It came up to Ken and started to sniff him from head to toe.

"Now, don't you worry, Amy, I'm not going to let this dog hurt you," said Ken. But no sooner had he said this than ...

"Chomp!" The dog bit and held Ken and tromped off up the sand hill.

Amy chased after the dog, scrambling up the sand hill.

Huffing, she made it to the top of the hill. From there she could see the ocean and hear the sound of the waves. Yet the dog and Ken were nowhere to be seen.

"Ken! Ken! Where are you?" shouted Amy, but her calls were drowned out by the sound of the waves.

Amy looked closely at the dog's footprints. Then, there in the sand, she could see that something was buried.

Amy quickly dug in the sand and soon Ken's head appeared.

Picking up Ken, Amy asked, "Ken, are you all right?"

"I'm all right. I'm all right," said Ken in a small voice.

"Look Ken, we can see the ocean from here," said Amy. But Ken responded only by saying, "I'm all right. I'm all right."

Carrying Ken on her back, Amy slid down the sand hill.

"Ken, where's Grandma's house?" asked Amy, but again
Ken only answered, "I'm all right. I'm all right."

By now, it was getting dark. Amy hurried towards the cluster of houses in the distance. There, down the road, Amy could see Grandma standing in front of her house.

Amy ran to Grandma.

"Grandma, can you fix Ken? Please, Grandma!"

"Don't worry Amy, Ken will be just fine. You did really well to come all the way here by yourselves, didn't you?" said Grandma. "Now, let's go inside."

"Dear, oh dear, Amy, Ken's legs are dangling and his arms are all frayed. And how in the world did he get such a flattened tail?" said Grandma, looking Ken over.

Sewing all his loose joints, Grandma said, "There, and now let me take a look at that flattened tail. I reckon a hot bath would be the best thing for that." But as soon as Ken heard the word "bath"…

… he jumped to his feet and started to run, crying,
"I don't want a bath! I've never had one and I never will!"

But Grandma caught Ken and plopped him in the bath.

"Ahh … this feels so good!" said Amy.

"So, Ken how do you like your first bath?"
asked Grandma.

"Well, at least it's better than being buried alive
in the cold sand," said Ken.

Drying off with a towel, Ken looked at his tail, all fluffy and clean now.

He looked and felt like a brand new fox. After staying two more nights with Grandma, Ken and Amy returned home.

"It was *so* good to see Grandma, wasn't it?" said Ken.

"Sure was!" said Amy.

Author/Illustrator

Born in Tokyo in 1945, **Akiko Hayashi** graduated from the Faculty of Fine Arts of Yokohama National University, after which she began working as a magazine illustrator. Her first children's book, *Miki's First Errand*, was published in 1973. Since then she has become one of Japan's leading picture book illustrators/writers, receiving numerous awards, domestic and international, for her outstanding work: The Second Japan Picture Book and Art Award for *I Love to Take Baths!*; and Le Grand Prix Des Treize for *I'm Going Camping* among many others. Titles written and illustrated by her include, *Amy and Ken Visit Grandma*, *Akiko Hayashi's Baby Diary*, *Who's in it?*, and *Yoshimi's Magic Colors*, as well as the Akiko Hayashi's Baby Book series and the Akiko Hayashi's Christmas Book series (all by Fukuinkan). Her books have been translated into more than ten languages. Ms. Hayashi resides in Tokyo.

Translators

Peter Howlett was born and raised in Hokkaido, Japan and currently teaches at Hakodate La Salle Junior and Senior High Schools. He lives near Hakodate and is married with three children.

Richard McNamara is a British-trained psychologist and a graduate of Kumanoto Graduate School of Education. He lives in Aso with his wife and family.

Together, Peter and Richard have translated a large number of Japan's classic children's picture books, including the Guri and Gura series, *Elephee's Walk*, *Miki's First Errand* and *Groompa's Kindergarten*.

R.I.C. Story Chest
こんとあき（英語版）
Amy and Ken Visit Grandma
2003年10月30日　初版発行

絵と文　林　明子
翻訳　　ピーター・ハウレット
　　　　リチャード・マクナマラ

発行者　ジョン・ムーア
発行所　アールアイシー出版株式会社
　　　　〒142-0051
　　　　東京都品川区平塚2-5-8
　　　　五反田ミカドビル5F
　　　　Tel. 03-3788-9201
　　　　Fax 03-3788-9202

　　　　ISBN　4-902216-01-9
　　　　Printed in Japan
　　　　http://www.ricpublications.com

Text and Illustrations © Akiko Hayashi 1989.

First published by Fukuinkan Shoten Publishers, Inc., Tokyo, Japan.

Re-published under licence by R.I.C. Publications Limited Asia, Tokyo, Japan

Japanese ISBN: 4 902216 01 9
International ISBN: 1 74126 014 0

Printed in Japan

Distributed by:

Asia
R.I.C. Publications – Asia
5th Floor, Gotanda Mikado Building,
2–5–8 Hiratsuka, Shinagawa-Ku Tokyo
Japan 142–0051
Tel: (03) 3788 9201
Email: elt@ricpublications.com
Website: www.ricpublications.com

Australasia
R.I.C. Publications
PO Box 332
Greenwood
Western Australia 6924
Tel: (618) 9240 9888

United Kingdom and Ireland
Prim-Ed Publishing
Bosheen
New Ross
Co. Wexford, Ireland
Tel: (353) 514 40075